# Koko the Monkey :

# Lost in Bangkok

THE ORIENTAL
BANGKOK SM

This edition printed exclusively
for The Oriental, Bangkok.

To my children,
the 3 J's,
with love.

First printed by Sirivatana Interprint, 2002
This edition printed 2005

Sirivatana Interprint Public Company Limited
Bangkok Thailand.

# Koko the Monkey :
## Lost in Bangkok

## Janice Santikarn
Illustrated by Prateep Paisarnnan

Deep in the jungle of Thailand lives Koko the baby monkey. His home is a tall tree, soft and warm. It is brown with long, shady green leaves and little round balls at the top. They are coconuts and Koko loves to eat the juicy white meat inside.

Koko picks a coconut from the tree and looks at it. How can he get it open? He thinks and thinks. After a while he hears a noise, "Toot-toot, toot-toot!" Koko looks down and sees a train. This gives him an idea!

Koko throws the coconut down. Down, down it falls. Finally, it hits the train and breaks open and out spills the juicy white meat.

Koko licks his lips and starts down the tree, climbing faster and faster until he slips and falls. Down, down, he falls......

....right on top of the train! The poor baby monkey hits his head and lies there completely still.

His eyes stay closed as the train races on through the jungle and carries him away.

A long time later, Koko wakes up. The train is now inside a big room. It is not the jungle and this is not his home. He must find his home!

Quickly he runs outside. He is at a railway station, the Hualamphong Railway Station.

He asks the Railway Station,

"Do I live here? Is this my home?"

But the Railway Station says,

"No. This is not your home."

"I am made of glass and cement and I am cold to touch but your home is soft and warm."

So Koko looks around. Parked by the side of a road is a little blue tuk-tuk. He runs to the tuk-tuk and climbs inside. It is soft and warm just like his home.

So he asks the tuk-tuk,
        "Do I live here? Is this my home?"
But the little blue tuk-tuk says,
        "No. This is not your home."
        "Your home is soft and warm like me but your home is also very tall. You must climb up high to get there."

So Koko gets down from the tuk-tuk and walks away. He walks past shops selling red lanterns, he walks past shops selling roast ducks and he walks past shops selling hats with long pigtails.

He is in Chinatown. Chinatown is not soft and warm and it is not tall. This is not his home. So he keeps walking.

Then all of a sudden he stops. In front of him is a white building and it is *very* tall. This is the Oriental Hotel. Koko runs to the hotel and gazes up. Up and up he looks.

He asks the Oriental Hotel,
        "Do I live here? Is this my home?"
But the Oriental Hotel says,
        "No, this is not your home."
        "Your home is very tall like me, but I am white and blue and your home is brown."

So Koko climbs down and goes on searching. He searches and searches. Then he stops, his eyes stare and his mouth drops open. In front of him stands a glittering, golden palace. It is the Grand Palace.

Koko goes inside and wanders around. He sees giant statues and beautiful temples but nothing tall and brown. Then he discovers a door. Slowly he pushes it open and suddenly there is water everywhere and the loud noise of motorboats. Koko is at a river, the Chao Phraya River.

He sees rice barges and ferry boats and,... yes!... something tall and brown. But it is on the other side of the river. Koko is puzzled. How can he get across?

Then he notices a long-tail boat speeding back and forth across the river and this gives him an idea. He runs to the edge of the water and jumps up on top of the boat. Soon the little monkey is at The Temple of the Dawn.

He asks the Temple of the Dawn,
     "Do I live here? Is this my home?"
But the Temple of the Dawn says,
     "No, this is not your home."
     "Your home is tall and brown like me, but your home is also green on top."

Koko is very sad now. He hangs his head and walks away. After a while, he feels tired and sits down near a large pond. There are turtles in the pond and they look happy in their home. Suddenly Koko's eyes are wet with tears. He wants *his* home  and he wants his mother!

Then the loud roar of car engines makes Koko sit up straight. He looks around and spots the cars, high up on a bridge. It is the Memorial Bridge and it is tall and brown ... and green on top too!

Suddenly Koko jumps up and wipes his tears away. He feels stronger now and rushes to the bridge.

He asks the Bridge,
"Do I live here? Is this my home?"
But the Bridge says,
"No, this is not your home."
"Your home is tall and brown like me. And your home is green up on top like me. But your home also has little round balls at the top."

Now Koko is happy. If he finds the little round balls then he will find his home. He looks around. Up on the bridge he can see for miles. Slowly, up and down the river he looks, and then he spies a bit of green!

He runs across the bridge and soon he is at the Flower Market. Here, there are red flowers, yellow flowers and white flowers, each with little green leaves. But there is nothing tall and brown and green and nothing with little round balls at the top. This is not his home.

So he keeps running. On and on he runs until he comes to a mountain, a huge golden mountain. He leaps upon the mountain and begins to climb, up and up, high above the city.

At the top of the Golden Mountain he looks down and smiles. In the distance he sees tall brown trees with green leaves and little round balls at the top.

Now Koko is really excited. He takes a deep breath and runs off. He runs and runs and soon he is at the Dusit Zoo.

He stops outside the front gate. He is very nervous and his heart is pounding. He wonders if he has finally found his home.

Eventually, Koko turns and goes inside. There he finds long-necked giraffes, tigers pacing back and forth in their cages, and big, heavy elephants.

And he finds monkeys! Many, many monkeys just like him. This must be his home! But how can he know for sure? He must ask someone.

Soon, Koko spots a very wise old coconut tree.
He asks the tree,
"Do I live here? Is this my home?"
But the Coconut Tree says,
"No, this is not your home."
"Your home is tall and brown, with big green leaves and little round balls at the top just like me. But you live in a jungle where there are many, many more trees like me."

"But where *is* the jungle?" asks Koko.
"It is very far away," explains the old tree. "Go to the river and find a boat. It will take you there."

Koko is *so* happy now. He thanks the tree and dashes off towards the river. He remembers the Oriental Hotel and he remembers the boats there. He will find one to take him home.

It is dark when baby Koko arrives at the hotel and there are many boats tied up at the pier. At last he finds the right one and quietly sneaks on board. Then he climbs into a hiding place and goes to sleep. While he sleeps the boat sails away.

Koko sleeps for a long time and dreams of his home in the jungle and of his mother.

Suddenly there is a bright light. Koko sits up and rubs his eyes. It is morning and the light is the sun.

He can see the jungle now but the boat is not stopping! He must get off ... but how? Then, up ahead, Koko sees a tree with a long branch hanging over the water. He smiles as he gets a brilliant idea.

When the boat sails under the branch, Koko springs up and grabs hold of it. Then he climbs onto the tree and hops down into the jungle.

Now there are tall trees all around him, just like the ones in the zoo. Finally this must be his home!

Suddenly Koko hears loud screeching and baby monkeys jump down onto the ground around him. There are many of them and he is frightened.

But then one big monkey steps forward and Koko smiles. All is quiet now as she holds out her arms to Koko and says, "I am your mother. And this is your home."

## ABOUT THE AUTHOR

Janice Santikarn was born in Australia, where she studied both Education and Chemistry. She worked as a Research Scientist in the U.S.A. before moving to Thailand in 1988. She taught English at a Thai Elementary School in Bangkok for several years before writing her first book, "*The Little Blue Tuk-tuk*". She is married and has 3 children.

## Other books by Janice Santikarn

*The Little Blue Tuk-tuk* by Janice Santikarn, illustrated by Sukit Tanmankong, Thai Watana Panich Press, Bangkok, 2000

*Nawin Saves the Elephants* by Janice Santikarn, illustrated by Rong Prapasanobon, Thai Watana Panich Press, Bangkok, 2000

*ABC of Thailand* by Janice Santikarn, illustrated by Janice Santikarn and Toni Skinner, Rung Silp Printing, Bangkok, 2002

*When I Grow Up (In Thailand)* by Janice Santikarn, illustrated by Sasawat Kayaroj, Sirivatana Interprint, Bangkok, 2003

*The Brave Little Tuk-Tuk* by Janice Santikarn, illustrated by Sukit Tanmankong, Sirivatana Interprint, Bangkok, 2004